D0471091

Walla Walla
County Libraries

MICHAEL GARLAND

SUPER SNOW DAY

SEEK AND FIND

Walla Walla County Libraries

Dutton Children's Books
an imprint of Penguin Group (USA) Inc.

To my wife, Peggy

DUTTON CHILDREN'S BOOKS
A division of Penguin Young Readers Group

Published by the Penguin Group
Penguin Group (USA) Inc., 375 Hudson Street, New York, New York 10014, U.S.A. • Penguin Group (Canada), 90 Eglinton Avenue East, Suite 700, Toronto, Ontario M4P 2Y3, Canada (a division of Pearson Penguin Canada Inc.) • Penguin Books Ltd, 80 Strand, London WC2R 0RL, England • Penguin Ireland, 25 St Stephen's Green, Dublin 2, Ireland (a division of Penguin Books Ltd) • Penguin Group (Australia), 250 Camberwell Road, Camberwell, Victoria 3124, Australia (a division of Pearson Australia Group Pty Ltd) • Penguin Books India Pvt Ltd, 11 Community Centre, Panchsheel Park, New Delhi—110 017, India • Penguin Group (NZ), 67 Apollo Drive, Rosedale, North Shore 0632, New Zealand (a division of Pearson New Zealand Ltd) • Penguin Books (South Africa) (Pty) Ltd, 24 Sturdee Avenue, Rosebank, Johannesburg 2196, South Africa • Penguin Books Ltd, Registered Offices: 80 Strand, London WC2R 0RL, England

Copyright © 2010 by Michael Garland
All rights reserved.
CIP Data is available.

Published in the United States by Dutton Children's Books, a division of Penguin Young Readers Group
345 Hudson Street, New York, New York 10014 • www.penguin.com/youngreaders

Designed by Beth Herzog

Manufactured in China • First Edition

ISBN: 978-0-525-42245-7
1 3 5 7 9 10 8 6 4 2

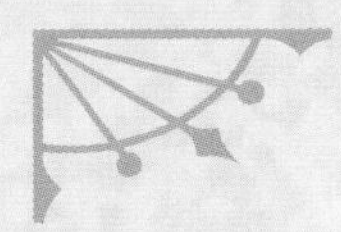
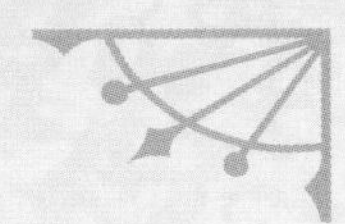

Dear Reader,

This book is a puzzle—
A hide-and-seek game.
You can hunt in the snow
For prizes to claim.

Winter sports symbols
Are placed here to find.
It won't be that easy;
It's a test of your mind.

Snowy titles throughout—
There are songs, poems, and books.
Just keep your eyes wide,
You'll find where to look.

On a walk in the woods
There are animals near.
But some sleep away
At this time of year.

Check the book's covers—
The front and the back.
So many things to discover,
So try and keep track.

Take a pencil and paper
And carefully look.
Make a list of the things
That you find in this book.

My list's at the end;
Take yours and compare.
If the two don't agree,
There's no need to despair.

Look again at these pages,
And as you go through,
You'll see if you're careful,
My numbers are true.

—Aunt Jeanne

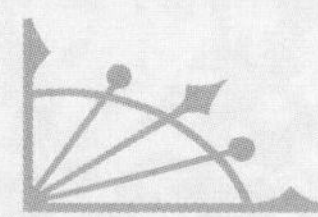

Tommy was about to eat his breakfast when he heard the TV news lady say, "The schools are closed! It's a snow day!"

Tommy looked into his cereal bowl and saw a note from his Aunt Jeanne.

Take a look out the window!
This is more than a flurry.
You have time on your hands now,
And not one single worry!

Tommy couldn't wait to get outside and have fun, but first he had to shovel the walk. He scooped up a note with his first shovel full of snow.

When you finish your work
You can come into town.
The world looks all new
When snow's coming down.

sneachta

CLEANERS
Snow Song
ALTERATIONS
SUITS
RUSH
WEDDING
COFFEE
DELI
neige

Tommy strapped on his snowshoes and trekked into town. The streets were alive with people enjoying the snowy day.

If you walk to town square,
You will see something smart.
You have to be crafty
To turn snow into art.

When Tommy reached the town square he saw a group of huge snow sculptures that people had made to celebrate their snow holiday. On the first one there was a note.

We've cleared off the whole lake.
Find a rod and some bait.
You might get a bite . . .
You just have to wait.

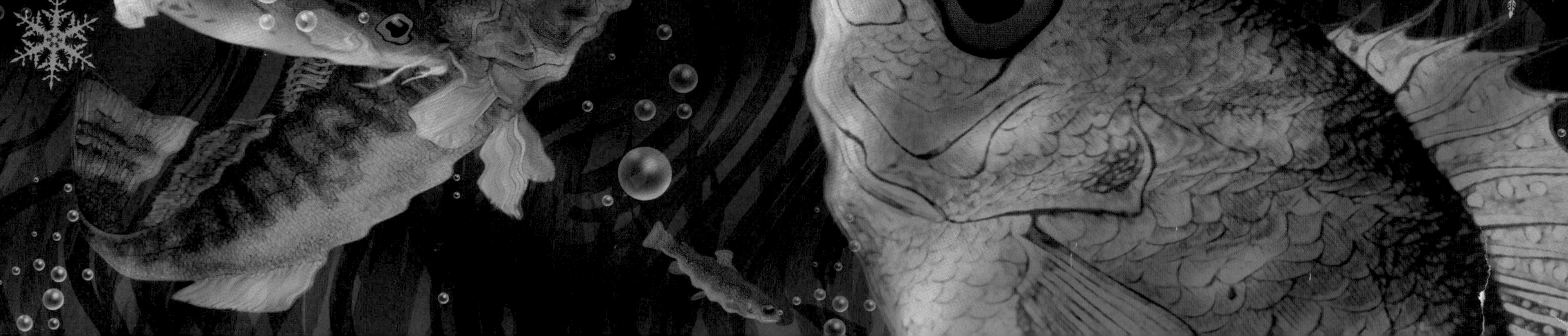

When he reached the lake, Tommy took off his snowshoes and joined the other ice fishers hoping to hook a big one. Across the lake an iceboat race was sailing past.

Tommy caught a big fish that had a note in its mouth.

Come join the crowd.
Go for a glide.
A sleigh and some horses
Make a nice winter ride.

Tommy followed the crowd going into the town park and took a ride on an old-fashioned sleigh. There was a note on his seat.

Take a stroll in the woods,
With the snow to your knees.
If you look closely,
You'll see more than trees.

THE SNOW QUEEN

neve

Footprints in the Snow

While Tommy was walking through the forest he noticed different animal tracks in the snow. Then he saw a note stuck to a thornbush.

Tommy looked into the mouth of the burrow. He could hear snoring. I wonder who is sleeping in there?

Just then a note came fluttering down with the snow.

A little Snow was here and there

снежок

Tommy continued his walk in the woods until he met Old Man Winter, Jack Frost, and the Abominable Snowman. Jack Frost handed Tommy a note.

It's a slippery slope,
But you'll give it a try.
Just don't stop your climbing,
Till you get to the sky!

Tommy came upon a band of climbers who were about to scale the side of an ice-covered mountain. They invited him to join them. When they reached the peak, he found a note stuck to an icicle.

Hey, hop on the back!
You're in for a thrill.
Before you know it
You've slid down the hill!

The Snowy Day

THE CROSS OF SNOW
schnee

At the top of the mountain, Tommy looked around and saw a bobsled race was just about to begin. The racers gave Tommy a helmet, and he climbed aboard. Then they took off down the mountain. There was a note stuck to the tail fin.

When you get to the bottom,
Try checking in for a day.
There's a frosty reception,
If you are planning to stay.

Snow-walker

ICE
PALACE
P

Tommy couldn't believe his eyes. Before him was a grand hotel made entirely of ice. On the front door there was a note.

Now go to the beach,
And see something cool!
Swimming in winter?
They'll say you're a fool!

The Snows of Kilimanjaro

The swimmers were having fun, so Tommy jumped right into the freezing water with them. He found a note frozen to the top of a bald man's head.

Come in from the cold
And warm yourself up.
I've got hot chocolate,
To fill up your cup!

Snowbird

눈

HAPPY S

NOW DAY
Let It Snow
sneeuw

Have you found everything there is to find?
Remember to look on the title page and the front and back covers!

Did you spot all of the animals in this book?
Don't forget the ones in the winter activity symbols! There are:

two rabbits, two blue jays, six horses, four cats, four dogs, two bears, one griffin, sixteen fish, one cardinal, one squirrel, one moose, one owl, one grouse, one fox, one raccoon, one bobcat, one turkey, one deer, one hedgehog, six mice, one badger, three bats, one lizard, two skunks, two frogs, two turtles, five chipmunks, two toads, one snake, and seven brown and red birds called *finches*.

Could you name all of the animals hibernating in Tommy's forest?

There are 27 hibernating animals in all, but just 12 different kinds of hibernators: hedgehog, mice, badger, bats, lizard, skunks, frogs, turtles, chipmunks, toads, snake, and bear.

There are nine different animal tracks in Tommy's forest.
Did you identify them all?

There are 17 symbols for fun winter sports and activities:

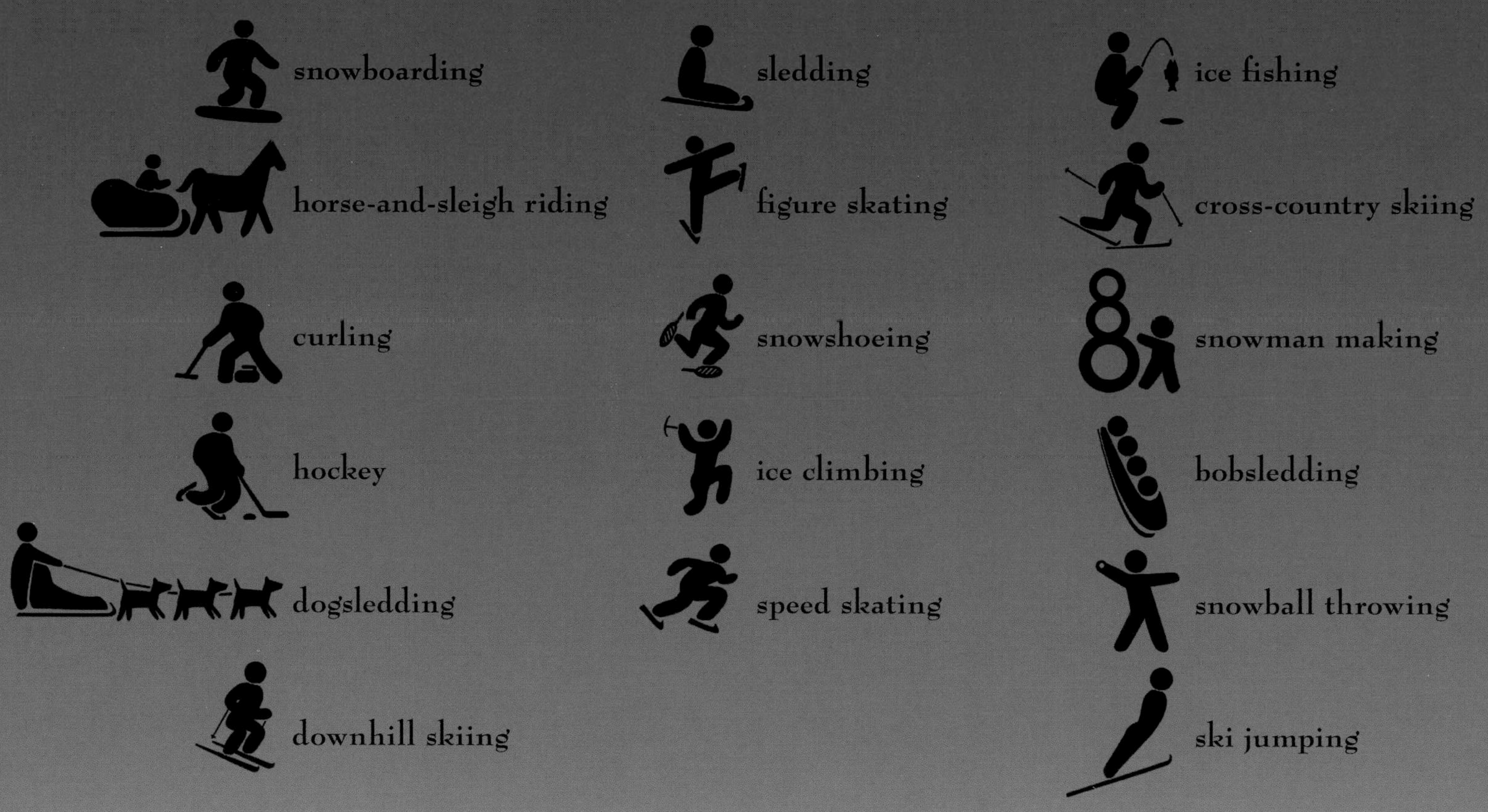

Did you find all of the words that mean "snow"? It appears in 16 languages.

Danish—sne

Eskimo—aput

Gaelic—sneachta

French—neige

Scots—snaw

Greek—χιόνι

Italian—neve

Spanish—nieve

Polish—śnieg

Russian—снежок

Tibetan—གངས་

German—Schnee

Finnish—lumi

Korean—눈

Dutch—sneeuw

Chinese—雪

There are 20 titles with the word "snow" in them—not counting the title of this book! Did you find them all?

"Snow Flakes" is a short story by Nathaniel Hawthorne.

From Snow to Snow is a collection of poetry by Robert Frost.

"Snow-Bound" is a poem by John Greenleaf Whittier.

Dream Snow is a picture book by Eric Carle.

Snowballs is a picture book by Lois Ehlert.

Snowflake Bentley is a picture book written by Jacqueline Briggs Martin and illustrated by Mary Azarian.

"Snow Song" is a song written by Brendan Milburn, Rachel Sheinkin, and Valerie Vigoda, performed by the band GrooveLily.

Edna St. Vincent Millay and Ralph Waldo Emerson both wrote poems called "The Snow Storm."

"Snow Geese" is a poem by Mary Oliver.

"The Snow Queen" is a fairy tale by Hans Christian Andersen.

"Footprints in the Snow" is a song by Bill Monroe and his Bluegrass Boys.

"A little Snow was here and there" is a poem by Emily Dickinson.

"Stopping by Woods on a Snowy Evening" is a poem by Robert Frost.

The Snowy Day is a picture book by Ezra Jack Keats.

"The Cross of Snow" is a poem by Henry Wadsworth Longfellow.

The Snow-walker is a novel by Catherine Fisher.

"The Snows of Kilimanjaro" is a short story by Ernest Hemingway.

"Snowbird" is a song by Gene MacLellan, performed by Anne Murray.

"Let it Snow" is a song by Sammy Cahn and Jule Styne.

"Snow White" is a story from *Grimm's Fairy Tales*.

Did you spot Aunt Jeanne in every scene?

She turns up seventeen times!

Did you count up all of the special six-pointed snowflakes?

There are 80 on the inside of the book and 31 on the front and back covers.
Don't forget to search the flaps of the book cover that fold in!

Did you find the letters that spell out HAPPY SNOW DAY?

There are hidden letters on pages 20, 14, 19, 26, 28, 8, 5, 11, 13, 6, 25 and 16.

Walla Walla County Libraries